NIGHT AT THE MUSEUM
BATTLE OF THE SMITHSONIAN

The Quest for the Golden Tablet

Adapted by A. J. Wilde
Based on the screenplay by
Robert Ben Garant & Thomas Lennon

HarperEntertainment
An Imprint of HarperCollinsPublishers

Library of Congress catalog card number: 2008944201
ISBN 978-0-06-171555-6
Book design by John Sazaklis
❖
First Edition

PROLOGUE: THE LEGEND OF THE GOLDEN TABLET

The Golden Tablet once belonged to the Pharaoh Ahkmenrah in ancient Egypt. Until recently, both the tablet and the tomb of Ahkmenrah were kept in the American Museum of Natural History in New York City. As Larry the Night Guard discovered, when the tablet's powers were used for good, they brought the exhibits in the museum to life. The historical figures lived and played together like a big family. But what would happen if the tablet's powers were ever used for evil . . . ?

When Larry decided to visit his old friends at the American Museum of Natural History, he was greeted by an alarming sight. Familiar exhibits were being boxed up!

Crates were being shipped to storage at the Smithsonian Museum in Washington, D.C. And that wasn't all: The historical figures were leaving *without* the Golden Tablet! "I'm afraid this night will be their last," Teddy Roosevelt said softly. The tablet brought the figures to life.

The next day, Larry got a phone call. His cowboy friend Jedidiah was calling from the Smithsonian. "The monkey stole the tablet, and now we're in a world of hurt! Kahmunrah, Ahkmenrah's big brother, is here and, trust me, *not friendly*!"

Dexter, the museum's sneaky monkey, had brought the tablet to Washington, D.C.! In Pharaoh Kahmunrah's evil hands, who knew what harm the tablet could cause? Larry knew what he had to do.

At the Smithsonian, Larry found a crate filled with his friends. With only a few minutes left before night fell, they had not come to life yet.

They were surrounded by six Egyptian warriors frozen in battle. Standing in front of them was the terrifying Pharaoh Kahmunrah. Larry found Dexter in a crate and pulled the tablet from his hands.

Night fell. Kahmunrah came to life and yelled, "Give me the tablet!"

Larry stood his ground.

"Hand it over, or I will kill you and your friends in the blink of an eye," the ruler threatened. Larry had no choice but to hand over the stone.

Kahmunrah fit the tablet into the gate, a portal to the Land of the Dead, and touched a combination of squares on its surface. "And now, my evil army of the damned shall . . . be . . . UNLEASHED!" Nothing happened.

"Mother and Father must have changed the combination," Kahmunrah whined.

Kahmunrah gave Larry the tablet and told him he had one hour to find the combination.

Larry remembered seeing Albert Einstein, a famous scientist, in the National Air and Space Museum. As he walked through the building, he came upon a monkey in a space suit who looked a lot like Dexter. His nametag said ABLE. As Larry knelt to take a closer look, the monkey came to life and snatched the tablet!

The descent stage comprised the lower part of the spacecraft and was an octagonal prism 4.2 meters across and 1.7 m thick. Four landing legs with round footpads were mounted on the sides of the descent stage and held the bottom of the stage 1.5 m above the surface.

The distance between the ends of the footpads on opposite landing legs was 9.4 m. One of the legs had a small astronaut egress platform and ladder. A one meter long conical descent engine skirt protruded from the bottom of the stage.

The descent stage contained the landing rocket, two tanks of aerozine 50 fuel, two tanks of nitrogen tetroxide oxidizer, water, oxygen and helium tanks and storage space for the lunar equipment and experiments, and in the case of Apollo 15, 16, and 17, the lunar rover.

The descent stage served as a platform for launching the ascent stage and was left behind on the Moon.

The ascent stage was an irregularly shaped unit approximately 2.8 m high and 4.0 by 4.3 meters in width mounted on top of the descent stage.

The ascent stage housed the astronauts in a pressurized crew compartment with a volume of 6.65 cubic meters which functioned as the base of operations for lunar operations. There was an ingress-egress hatch in one side and a docking hatch for connecting to the CSM on top.

Also mounted along the top were a parabolic rendezvous radar antenna, a steerable parabolic S-band antenna, and 2 in-flight VHF antennas.

Two triangular windows were above and to either side of the egress hatch and four thrust chamber assemblies were mounted around the sides.

At the base of the assembly was the ascent engine. The stage also contained an aerozine 50 fuel and an oxidizer tank, and helium, liquid oxygen, gaseous oxygen, and reaction control fuel tanks.

There were no seats in the LM. A control console was mounted in the front of the crew compartment above the ingress-egress hatch and between the windows and two more control panels mounted on the side walls. The ascent stage was launched from the Moon at the end of lunar surface operations and returned the astronauts to the CSM.

Larry chased Able into an exhibit of the moon landing. He jumped—and floated in the air! The exhibit didn't have much gravity, just like the moon, and Larry bounced around slowly as he tried to follow Able. "Bad space monkey. No!" Larry grabbed the tablet.

Larry got the combination from Albert Einstein and brought the tablet back to the evil king. "Open the crate and release my friends," ordered Larry. But Kahmunrah had already gotten the code! The tablet glowed, and the gate opened. Out came a terrifying army of man-birds, the Horus soldiers, who let out ear-piercing squawks and raised their spears.

Larry prepared for battle with his brave old friends—along with some new ones from the Smithsonian, including the fearless pilot Amelia Earhart. Just then, a window shattered and in walked Abraham Lincoln! He charged toward the Horus soldiers, who ran, terrified, back through the gate.

Now Larry and Kahmunrah fought one-on-one.

Larry knocked the sword out of Kahmunrah's hand with his flashlight.

"Who *are* you?" Kahmunrah asked in amazement.

"I'm the Night Guard," Larry replied, as he kicked the pharaoh in the stomach and sent him flying through the gate. Larry shut the gate and took the tablet out of the door.

Now, Larry had to get the exhibits, and the tablet, back to the American Museum of Natural History, where they truly belonged.

"Miss Earhart, think you could hook us up with a ride?"

Amelia smiled.

Larry couldn't wait to get back to the museum and make everything right again.

Back in New York, Teddy was relieved to see Larry and his friends. "I extend to you a hearty well-done, lad," Teddy said.

Larry became a Night Guard once again. "Well, clearly the world works in mysterious ways," said Larry's boss, McPhee. "One day, we're getting rid of everything old; the next, some rich, anonymous donor gives the museum a ton of money on the condition that everything stay the same."

But things weren't exactly the same. The museum was now open late, and tour groups were being led by "live" exhibits.

"Whoa!" Three teenage boys screamed in shock as Rexy stood up and roared in their faces.

"Honestly, today's technology is beyond me," said McPhee.
"Yeah, it's . . . something else," answered Larry, who knew the "technology" was really the magic of the Golden Tablet—finally back where it belonged.